S0-ANQ-958

Published by Modern Publishing
A Division of Unisystems, Inc.

Copyright © - 1988 Modern Publishing, a division of Unisystems, Inc.

™ - Lullababies is a trademark owned by Modern Publishing, a division of
Unisystems, Inc.

® - Honey Bear Books is a trademark owned by Honey Bear Productions, Inc.,
and is registered in the U.S. Patent and trademark office.

No part of this book may be reproduced or copied without written permission
from the publisher.

All Rights Reserved.

Printed in Singapore

Favorite Lullabies

to read aloud

illustrated by J. Ellen Dolce   edited by Bill Gutman

MODERN PUBLISHING
A Division of Unisystems, Inc.
New York, New York 10022

Brahms' Lullaby

Lullaby and good night,
With roses bedight
With lilies bedecked
Is baby's wee bed;
Lay thee down now and rest,
May thy slumber be blessed.
Lay thee down now and rest,
May thy slumber be blessed.

Rock-A-Bye Baby

Rock-a-bye baby on the tree top,
When the wind blows the cradle will rock,
When the bough breaks the cradle will fall,
And down will come baby, cradle and all.

Sweet and Low

Sweet and low, sweet and low,
Wind of the western sea;
Low, low, breathe and blow,
Wind of the western sea!
Over the rolling waters go,
Come from the dying moon and blow,
Blow him again to me,
While my little one,
While my pretty one,
Sleeps.

Sleep and rest, sleep and rest,
Father will come to thee soon;
Rest, rest, on mother's breast,
Father will come to thee soon.
Father will come to his babe in the nest,
Silver sails all out of the west,
Under the silver moon.
Sleep, my little one,
Sleep, my pretty one,
Sleep.

—Alfred Tennyson

Mozart's Lullaby

Sleep, baby, sleep, and good night,
All the birds are asleep and out of sight,
Quiet the lambs on the hill,
Even the bumblebees are still.
Only the man in the moon
Is still nodding, but soon
Over him slumber will creep,
Sleep, baby, sleep, go to sleep.
Good night,
Good night.

To Babyland

How many miles to babyland?
Anyone can tell;
Up one flight and to your right;
Don't forget to ring the bell.

What do they do in babyland?
They dream and wake and play;
They laugh and crow, and fonder grow.
Jolly times have they.

Oh Slumber, My Darling

Oh slumber, my darling,
Thy sire is a knight,
Thy mother is a lady,
So lovely and bright.
The hills and the dales
From the towers which we see,
Shall one day belong,
My sweet infant to thee.
Oh, rest thee, Babe, rest thee Babe
Sleep while you may.

Bedtime

The evening is coming, the sun sinks to rest,
The crows are all flying straight home to their nests.
"Caw," says the crow as he flies over head,
It's time little people were going to bed.

The flowers are dozing,
The daisies are asleep.
The primroses are buried in slumber so deep.
Closed for the night are the roses so red,
It's time little people were going to bed.

Bye Baby Bunting

Bye baby bunting,
Daddy's gone a-hunting,
Off to get a rabbit skin,
To wrap his baby bunting in.

The Sandman Comes

The sandman comes, the sandman comes,
With such pretty snow-white sand,
For he is known throughout the land,
The sandman comes.

Sleep, Baby, Sleep

Sleep, baby, sleep;
Thy father is watching the sheep,
Thy mother is shaking the dreamland tree,
And down falls a little dream on thee,
Sleep, baby, sleep.
Sleep, baby, sleep.

Sleep, baby, sleep;
The large stars are the sheep,
The little stars are the lambs, I guess,
And the bright moon is the shepherdess.
Sleep, baby, sleep.
Sleep, baby, sleep.

Hush, Little Baby

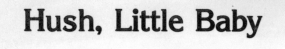

Hush, little baby, don't say a word,
Mama's gonna buy you a mockingbird.
And if that mockingbird don't sing,
Mama's gonna buy you a diamond ring.
And if that diamond ring turns to brass,
Mama's gonna buy you a looking glass.
And if that looking glass gets broke,
Mama's gonna buy you a billy goat.

And if that billy goat won't pull,
Mama's gonna buy you a cart and bull.
And if that cart and bull turn over,
Mama's gonna buy you a dog named Rover.
And if that dog named Rover won't bark,
Mama's gonna buy you a horse and cart.
And if that horse and cart fall down,
You'll still be the sweetest little baby in town.

The Linden Tree

A linden tree is standing
Beside a running stream;
I lay beneath its shadows
And dreamed a happy dream.

The rustling of its branches
Was like a lullaby;
I listened to its stories,
As I watched the clouds go by.

A Fairy Lullaby

Oh, I wish I were a fairy,
With a pair of silver wings,
And a lot of shining stardust in my hair.
I would frolic with the butterflies,
And bees and flying things,
And I'd dine upon the daintiest of fare.

I would sup upon a dewdrop
And I'd sleep within a rose,
Only to be awakened by a droning bumblebee.
And if I should chance to tumble,
Off into another doze,
There would not be a single soul to see.

The Sandman

The flowers have gone to beddy,
The moon has begun to shine,
Each nods its little headdy
Upon its stem so fine.
The branches rustle;
And they seem to sigh, as in a dream.
Sleepy, sleepy, sleepy,
Sleep, my baby, sleep.

The birds that sing so sweetly by day,
Have gone to rest,
And each is tucked up neatly,
All in its little nest,
The cottage in the garden here
Is still awake, I fear.
Sleepy, sleepy, sleepy,
Sleep, my baby, sleep.

The Sandman will be coming
And poking in his head,
To look for naughty children
That haven't gone to bed;
And if he takes them by surprise,
The sand flies in their eyes.
Sleepy, sleepy, sleepy,
Sleep, my baby, sleep.

Twinkle, Twinkle, Little Star

Twinkle, twinkle, little star—
How I wonder what you are!
Up above the world so high,
Like a diamond in the sky.
Twinkle, twinkle, little star—
How I wonder what you are!

—Jane Taylor

The Land of Nod

From breakfast on through all the day
At home among my friends I stay,
But every night I go abroad
Afar into the land of Nod.

All by myself I have to go,
With none to tell me what to do—
All alone beside the streams
And up the mountain-sides of dreams.

The strangest things are there for me,
Both things to eat and things to see,
And many frightening sights abroad
Till morning in the land of Nod.

—Robert Louis Stevenson